Our Little Turkish Cousin

Mary Hazelton Blanchard Wade

Our Little Turkish Cousin

CHAPTER I

OSMAN

Of course Osman cannot remember his first birthday. He is a big boy now, with brown eyes and soft, dark hair. Ten years have rolled over his head since he lay in the little cradle by the side of his mother's grand bedstead.

He made an odd picture,—this tiny baby in cotton shirt and quilted dressing-gown. His head was encased in a cap of red silk. A tassel of seed-pearls hung down at one side. Several charms were fastened to the tassel. His mother thought they would keep harm and danger away from this precious baby boy.

He could not have felt very comfortable. His nurse had straightened out his arms and legs, and bound them tightly with bandages. After dressing him, she placed him in his little bed and covered him with several quilted wrappers. Last of all, a thin, red veil was spread over this little Turkish baby.

Do you think he could have enjoyed himself very much? I don't.

He was ready for visitors now. First of all, the proud and delighted father must come in to see his child. A boy, too! The grave man was doubly pleased when he thought of this. As he looked for the first time upon the tiny form done up in so many wrappers, he could hardly tell whether the boy was big or little, fat or thin.

He bent down over the cradle and lifted the child into his own strong arms. Holding him tenderly, he carried him from the room. He stopped just outside the door. There he stood for a few moments while he repeated a short prayer and whispered the name "Osman" three times in the baby's ear.

This was the only christening the Turkish boy would ever receive. Osman would be his name for the rest of his life; and a fine name it was, his mother and friends all agreed.

When the baby was three days old, there was a grand celebration at his home.

Certain old women, called "bringers of tidings," went from one house to another where the lady friends of Osman's mother had their homes. Wherever they stopped, these old women left bottles of sherbet made of sugar-candy, spices, and water. As they presented the sherbet, they told of the good news about the new baby, of the name his father had given him, and of the feast to be held at Osman's home.

"Do come, do come. You will surely be welcome. You will be glad to see the child and rejoice with his mother."

In this way the invitations were given; and so it happened that many ladies found their way to Osman's house on the day named. No special hour was set for their visit. But, from morning till night, people were coming and going.

It was easy enough for passers-by to know something of interest was taking place inside. They could hear the band of music playing lively airs as the ladies drove up to the door and entered the house.

All the visitors wore long cloaks, with veils over their faces, hiding everything except their soft, dark eyes. For it is still the fashion in Turkey that no lady shall be seen away from her home with her face uncovered.

Very few of these visitors came alone. They were attended by their slaves and servants, laden with baskets. These baskets were very pretty. They were trimmed with flowers and ribbons, and filled with all sorts of delicious sweets.

Of course they were presents for the new baby's mother. She lay in her grand state bed, smiling softly as the ladies came up, one by one, to greet her. Before they entered her chamber, they took off their veils and cloaks in an outside room.

"Mashallah! May the child live long and be happy," said the visitors, as they bent over the young mother. At each kind wish, she kissed the hands of the speaker. This was her way of thanking them. Strange to say, the ladies seemed hardly to notice the baby himself, in whose honour they had come to the house.

Do not think for a moment they had forgotten the tiny bundle done up in quilted cotton. No, indeed. But the anxious mother believed some bad fortune might come to Osman if he were examined too closely. She would worry if her friends should fondle the child or pay him much attention.

This is the reason most of them pretended not to see him. A few, however, were so curious they could not resist stopping for a moment at the cradle. But, instead of saying, "Oh, the darling little fellow!" or, "What a bright-looking child!" or other kind words, they exclaimed, "The ugly little creature!" "What stupid eyes he has!" or some such unpleasant thing.

Would you believe it? Osman's mother seemed really pleased as she listened. She said to herself, "Well, if they praised my child, I should think they were trying to hide some bad wish. That very wish would bring an accident to my darling, sooner or later. No, I like best to hear them speak as they do. I know they do not mean what they say."

The visitors were in no hurry to leave Osman's home. They made themselves comfortable on the soft couches. They laughed and chatted together while they ate ices and rich cakes, and sipped coffee or sherbet.

The refreshments were of many kinds, for the baby's father was rich and held a high office under the Sultan, as the ruler of Turkey is called.

If Osman had been born in a poor family, his parents would have had a celebration just the same. The feast would not have been as rich, but coffee and fruits would have been served, at any rate, and the visitors would probably have enjoyed themselves just as much.

When Osman was eight days old, there was another great ceremony at his house. He received a bath. The ladies who were invited could join in the bath if they liked, as well as his mother. There would be music and refreshments and a general good time.

The baby was bathed first. His mother's turn came next.

A Turkish bath is not like that of other people, as perhaps you have heard. A long time is spent before it is finished. On this great day in Osman's life, it was even longer than usual. Many songs were sung, and the visitors stopped several times to eat refreshments.

All this sounds odd to us, but the rich ladies of Turkey have little to do except to ride and make calls, bathe in their own homes or at the public bath-houses, meet together for picnics or some entertainment.

Osman grew so fast it seemed to his mother only a short time before he was able to toddle about without the help of his nurse. The carpets were soft and thick, so he did not get hurt even if he fell. The beautiful colours of the carpets amused his baby eyes.

He was awake every morning soon after sunrise, but this did not trouble his parents. They were early risers, too. The boy's father liked to have plenty of time for sipping coffee and smoking his pipe before leaving home for the day.

There was no such thing as breakfast. The family ate only two real meals in the whole day. But the early morning was a pleasant time. There was no jumping up from the table after a hasty meal. There was no rushing for the train after a hurried kiss and goodbye to wife and baby. Oh, no, none of these things are done in Turkey.

Osman's father dressed himself in a comfortable, loose gown, and seated himself cross-legged on a rug. He clapped his hands and a slave appeared with the steaming coffee, which was placed on a low stand near by. Then the baby's mother poured out the coffee and, handing it to her husband, sat down on a cushion at his feet.

Osman, still in his nightclothes, toddled about, nibbling a sweet-cake.

The slave who had brought the coffee was now busy in tidying the room. First of all, mattresses and wadded coverlets must be stowed away in a cupboard. There was no bedstead. Such a clumsy piece of furniture had been used in the house but once. That was when the young mother lay in state to receive her friends when Osman was born.

Would you believe it! the baby's mother was still wearing her wadded night-dress. She often kept it on for hours after she got up in the morning.

"It is so comfortable," she thought. "Why should I hurry to dress myself for the day?"

After the coffee, the father took his pipe and lighted it with a tiny piece of charcoal. Now for a comfortable smoke. As he puffed away at his pipe, the room was quiet except for little Osman's prattle. He was trying to tell his father and mother about his play-things.

After a while the sober Turk laid down his pipe, and said, "It is time for business."

The dressing-gown was taken off, and street clothes were put on. What a grand-looking gentleman he was now, with his long beard hanging over his snow-white shirt-front, his embroidered vest, and wide, loose trousers.

He lifted Osman up for a kiss, and, with a deep bow to his wife, he left home for the day.

CHAPTER II

SCHOOL

"Mamma, mamma, I am so glad it has come at last!" said little Osman, early one bright spring morning.

"Yes, yes, my darling," answered his mother. "It is a good time; I am glad, too."

What made Osman wake up sooner than usual this morning? What caused his eyes to look so bright? Why was the nurse taking such pains with his hair and dress?

He was going to school for the first time in his life. His sixth birthday had come and gone, and his father had said:

"It is time for my little boy to do something besides play. He must learn to read our good books, and understand the use of numbers."

The important day was set and the teacher was told about the new pupil. Word was also sent to the priest.

Osman's father spent some time in choosing a pony on which his boy should first ride to school. At last he decided on one of an iron-gray colour and very handsome.

"What beautiful trappings!" exclaimed Osman, when the pony arrived at the door. "Oh, you dear, kind father to get them!"

Any boy would be pleased to ride on a pony decked out in such a gay manner.

The pony had no sooner arrived than the whole school appeared at the door. The children were dressed in their best clothes to do honour to the new pupil.

The priest took his place in front of the young company. They instantly bent low while he made a short prayer. After this, Osman was lifted to the back of the pony, the other children formed in double line, and the procession started out for the school.

But it did not move quietly. Hymn after hymn was sung by the little ones in strong, clear voices as they went along.

The grown-ups whom they passed smiled and said to themselves, "A child is on his way to school for the first time. It is a glad day. May he grow wise and be happy."

What an odd-looking schoolroom it was that Osman soon entered; neither seats nor desks could be seen. Three divans, as the big, soft Turkish couches are called, stood along the wall. The children squatted cross-legged on these, side by side.

After they had taken their places, the teacher sat down in front of his little class and began to hear their lessons.

Each child had by this time opened his book and begun to recite. Not one of them at a time. Oh, no, indeed! They spoke together in high, sharp voices. How could the schoolmaster understand what they said?

He did not seem to have any trouble, however, and kept the children busy. They read from the Koran, which is the sacred book of their people, they recited numbers, and they wrote.

You remember they had no desks. The poor little things had to hold their copy-books in their laps, and it was tiresome work. Their pens were made of reeds, and sponges took the place of ink-wells.

Before the children were dismissed, the master told them a story which interested Osman very much.

Osman kneeling on floor in front of grandmother OSMAN AND HIS MOTHER.
"I will repeat it to my mother," he said to himself. "The story teaches us not to seem surprised, no matter what may happen. My father has spoken of this very thing. It is not polite to be astonished. That is what he has often said."

As the little boy rode homeward, he saw a man sitting cross-legged at the street corner. Two veiled women stood in front of him. They were eagerly watching the man as he wrote. From time to time he stopped as one of the women told him something more she wished him to put into the letter.

"He is a street scribe," thought Osman. "They will pay him for that letter. They do not know how to write. That is why they get him to do it. How quickly he makes the letters, and how easily he holds his pen. I hope it won't be long before I can write as well as he does."

Such a scribe is often seen in the streets of Constantinople, the city where Osman lives. There are many people there who can neither read nor write. Fine ladies are not ashamed to stop at a scribe's little stand and ask him to write letters for them, as these people were doing.

Osman's school was only a short distance from home, and he was soon at his own gate. The moment he arrived, the door was opened by an old black slave, who had been watching for the darling of the house.

"I'd like to stop and tell you what I've been doing this morning, but I can't now," said Osman. "I must tell mother first."

The little boy ran up the stairs to his mother's rooms. In another moment he was seated on a divan beside her and talking faster than one often hears among the quiet people of his country.

Lunch was soon brought, and, you may be sure, the little boy was ready for it. There was a dish of pilaf, of course. It was made of nicely cooked rice and butter, and was delicious. Then there was a juicy melon, and fresh figs, besides cakes sweetened with honey, candy, and many other nice things.

Osman's mother is as fond of sweet things as her little boy, and she is ready to eat them at any time. The lunch was served at an odd little table. Indeed, it could hardly be called a table,—it was a small, low stand, about eight inches above the floor. The dishes were brought in one at a time, and placed on the stand.

Osman and his mother ate the pilaf with their fingers, from the same dish. But they did not hurry. The grains of rice were picked up so daintily with their finger-tips, they were hardly soiled by the touch of the food.

"We will wash now," Osman's mother said, as the lunch was finished. A queer basin was at once brought by a servant, and held in front of the lady. In the middle of the basin was a little stand holding a cake of soap, while underneath was a sort of well. This was to receive the water as it left the basin. As

Osman's mother held out her hands, one servant slowly poured the water over them, while another held an embroidered towel ready for her use.

It was Osman's turn next. No matter how much he wished to hurry out to play, he must not rise from his cushion till his hands were bathed.

"Wash before eating and afterward," is a law of the Koran. Osman thinks it would be as wicked to break this rule as to tell a wrong story, or take anything belonging to another.

As soon as the hand-washing was over, the little boy started for the courtyard to watch his tame pigeons and play with his friend Selim.

Osman's house is divided into two parts. His father's rooms are down-stairs. A separate door leads into them from the street. No woman ever enters these rooms. Even the servants who take care of them are men. The boy's father receives his gentlemen friends in this part of the house. It is here that he talks over business with his visitors. Sometimes he holds dinner-parties in these rooms, but they are only for men. He even has a separate courtyard and garden. Osman may come here if he likes, but the real home of the family is up-stairs in his mother's rooms.

This part of the house is very beautiful. Rich curtains hang in the doorways. Soft and heavy rugs are placed here and there on the floors. Divans with soft cushions stretch along the sides of the walls, under the latticed windows.

Yes, every window is covered with lattice-work, so that no one passing along the street below can see the faces of the persons within these upper rooms.

This is the fashion of the country. Poor women of Turkey! They seem to us almost like prisoners, but they have been brought up to think of their life as the most natural and best in the world. They may go outdoors whenever they like, so long as a veil is worn over the face. But no man, unless he is a very near relative, must enter the part of the house where the women and children have their home.

CHAPTER III

THE FIRE

"Listen, listen, Osman. What is all the noise about?" exclaimed Selim. It was toward the end of the afternoon, and both boys were growing tired of play.

"It's a fire. Don't you see the police? They are hurrying along with pails of water on their heads. Then, look quickly down the street! Smoke is coming out of that building. Let's ask nurse to go with us."

In another moment Osman had run into the house and out again, with old black Fatima trotting after as fast as she could move. She hurriedly pulled her veil over her face. Then, taking each boy by the hand, she led them through the gate, and joined the crowd of people who were going in the direction of the fire.

Everybody looked gay and happy. Why shouldn't they have a good time? The fire did not happen through any fault of theirs. It would be a grand sight, and the onlookers might as well enjoy it.

There were no fire-engines in the city. The policemen brought pails of water, but these did little good.

And now, not only columns of smoke are bursting through the windows and doorways, but flames are leaping and dancing along the openings. See! Those who are still inside the burning house are throwing out cushions and mats, curtains and pillows, into the street. Such furnishings can be saved, even if the building is destroyed.

The watching crowd seize these articles and at once make themselves comfortable. A number of women sit down on a pile of soft rugs and prepare to enjoy the show, as if they were at the theatre. Not far off is a group of men, who stand chatting and smoking. The balconies of neighbouring houses are filled with gazing crowds.

The street peddlers soon begin to arrive. They bring trays of sweetmeats, sherbets, and other good things. As they elbow their way through the crowd, they act as though the fire had been started on purpose to give them a chance to sell their goods.

Still the fire rages; the timbers creak; the walls begin to totter; the roof gives way, and falls inward with a crash. In a few moments more, only a heap of charred wood is left in the place of a fine house.

It might have been saved if firemen could have been here with their engines. But they are unknown, as yet, in this great city of the Turks, where many buildings are destroyed by fire every year.

"Come, come, children," said Fatima, "it is late. The shadows are beginning to fall. Osman, your father is surely home by this time and will wonder where you are."

While the old woman hurried the boys along, they ate fig-paste they had bought of a peddler.

No doubt you, children of other lands, have eaten fig paste, too. But perhaps you have never thought of the people who invented it. It is a Turkish sweetmeat, and Osman thinks it is delicious when freshly made by a candy merchant in his city.

"The fire has waked up every dog in this quarter," said Fatima, fretfully, as she hurried the children along. She was right in saying so, for "Bow-wow-wow, bow-wow-wow," could be heard in every direction. Even as she spoke, the old nurse stumbled against a big dog that was rushing past her and barking furiously.

"Hurry up, old fellow! Catch him, catch him!" cried Osman, turning around to watch. "Fatima, don't you see what is the matter? He is driving a strange dog out of the street. I hope he will succeed."

Just as Osman spoke, a half-dozen other dogs came tearing along, eager to join in the chase. There was small chance for the stranger, who was now running with all his might. His tongue was hanging from his mouth, and his tail was thrashing from side to side between his legs.

Poor homeless dogs of Constantinople! There are thousands of them. Yes, it is the very truth. There are scores of thousands of them.

Those big, gaunt, yellow creatures live in the streets and byways, under the door-steps and in the graveyards. They feed on the garbage thrown out from the kitchens, but sometimes get a little choicer food through the kindness of the people.

"Kill a dog without real need of doing so! No, no," Osman's father would say, very solemnly. "It is the law of our religion that we should kill nothing living if we can possibly help it. Let the dogs live.

"Besides, they are useful creatures. They keep our streets clean of all decaying matter. By doing this, fevers and many other kinds of illness are prevented. The poor animals are a real blessing."

"I know where there are some new-born puppies," said Selim, as he was leaving Osman for the night.

"Where? Let's go and see them now. Is it near here?" cried his little friend.

"Yes, it's only a few steps."

"No, no, children," broke in Fatima, "you ought to be in your own homes this very moment. Wait till morning, and I will go with you before school-time."

"Are their eyes open yet? Does their mother seem fond of them? How many are there?" asked Osman.

But Fatima did not give Selim a chance to answer. She had already rung the bell at the door of his house, and a servant had appeared to take charge of him.

So, without stopping for anything except a kind wish to Selim for his peace and happiness, she led her own little charge home. His father had reached there before him, and was all ready to talk over the day's doings with his only child.

As the Turk sat smoking that evening, Osman described the fire he had seen, and told of the hunted dog he had met on the way home.

"He ought to have known better than to come into a strange quarter," said the boy. "It was all he could expect. Any dog that remains at home is not troubled by the others. I love the creatures; don't you, papa? They are gentle and quiet and clever."

"Yes, Osman, the city would not seem like home without our yellow-haired dogs. Before you were born, however, the Sultan thought it would be wise to clear our streets of them. Great numbers were taken to an island near the coast."

"Did they die there from want of food, papa?"

"Oh, no. They were too wise to stay there and starve. They all swam back to the city. Our people were so pleased, the dogs have never been troubled since then."

"I love the dogs because they are not only gentle, but they do not forget a kindness. They are grateful creatures," said Osman's mother. "I have a friend who told me the story of an English lady living here in our city. She had a small terrier she had brought back with her after a visit to England.

"I suppose, Osman, you know that our dogs are always ready to attack one of a different breed?"

"Yes, mamma."

"Well, it happened one day that this little terrier escaped from his home and got out into the street among the dogs of the city."

"Did they kill him?"

"No, indeed. But they had a reason for being friendly to him. The English lady and her family had always been kind to them, and had often fed them. Not only this, but she had seen that pans of water were placed in the street on hot days, so the dogs should not suffer from thirst. They were grateful to her, and seemed to feel that her pet terrier was also a friend.

"After this, the lady allowed her dog to play with the others as much as he liked. He was always well treated. But he did not have sense enough to keep in his own street One day he wandered off into another quarter, and he was instantly attacked. His dog friends heard the noise and rushed after him. When they got to him, he was surrounded on all sides by his enemies.

"It would have gone hard with him, if one brave friend had not seized him by the neck and rushed home with him. He did not stop till he reached the lady's house, where he dropped the terrier on the door-step.

"Even then, he and his comrades did not go away. There they waited till the owner appeared, when they tried to explain, as well as poor doggies can, what had happened."

"What noble fellows they were," said Osman, when his mother had finished the story. "I shall love them more than ever." Then the little boy went on to tell of the family of puppies Selim had discovered.

"I will go to see them early to-morrow morning, and will carry some food to the mother," he said. "I love puppies. They are beautiful little things, and their hair is as soft as silk."

Osman loved pets as much as any other boy in the wide world, and he was always ready to take a family of puppies into his heart. His parents taught him, however, that it was not good to handle them. "The dog is an unclean animal," said the boy's father. "Be kind to him and love him, but touch him as little as possible."

CHAPTER IV

THE PICNIC

It was a beautiful summer day. The sun was shining brightly on the glossy leaves of the olive-trees in Osman's garden, and the plants were loaded with blossoms.

Osman had just picked a bunch of flowers when he heard his mother's voice.

"How would you like a day by the Sweet Waters of Europe, my child?"

The little boy looked in the direction of the voice. His mother was moving slowly down the garden path.

"That would be lovely, mamma, but can't Selim go with us?"

"Certainly, and I have sent word to some of my friends to join us, too. We will have a merry time. I am tired of the house, and I long for a row on the beautiful river. Let Fatima go for Selim, and make yourself ready at once."

The little boy's mother was already dressed for the excursion. So, while the servants were preparing the lunch and Osman was getting ready, she sat down on a cushion under the trees and idly waited.

She was richly clad in a pink silk mantle with wide sleeves and deep cape. It was so long it reached down to her ankles.

A small, bright-coloured cap, trimmed with pearls, was fitted closely to her head. The thin muslin veil, fastened to this cap, was brought around her face so no part of it could be seen except her soft, kind eyes.

She did not have long to wait before her friends and Selim arrived to join in the day's outing. The slaves, with wraps and carpets, were also ready, and, at a sign from their mistress, the party started out.

How queerly the ladies walked! They waddled along in a clumsy fashion with their skirts tucked up under their mantles and around their waists. They looked like shapeless bundles moving along in loose trousers and clumsy overshoes.

17

It was only a few steps to the waterside, where boats were waiting for them. The boatmen first helped the ladies to get in and seat themselves on soft cushions; next came the two boys, and, last of all, the servants.

When every one was comfortably settled, and umbrellas had been raised over the ladies' heads to protect them from the strong sunlight, the men bent to their oars and they were off.

The boats were light and very graceful. They were of a kind the Turks call kaiks. They sped onward through the water as the men gave long, strong pulls at the oars.

On and on they went, now rapidly as the river widened; again, they moved more slowly as they entered a narrow stretch of water, almost filled with the boats of other pleasure-seekers.

Sometimes they were obliged to pass under a little wooden bridge. Then it was fun for Osman and Selim to reach up and see if they could touch the floor of the bridge before they left it behind them.

Pretty houses stood here and there on the banks of the river, or groves of trees that seemed to say, "Stop here and rest awhile. I will give you shade and comfort."

But still the rowers kept on, as though their arms would never get tired. They did not speak, these sober-faced men. Each wore a red fez on his head, which made him look hot and uncomfortable in the strong sunshine.

There was a time when all Turks wore soft turbans, which are the best and most comfortable covering for the head. But times are changed now. The great Sultan likes the fez best, and the turban is seen more and more seldom as the years pass by.

At last the party reached a spot where Osman's mother decided to stop. It was a favourite picnic-ground for the people of Constantinople. A pretty grove of trees was growing close to the shore, while, near by, tiny coffee-houses stood here and there in the meadows.

"I hear sweet music," said Osman. "Listen, mamma."

"Yes, it is a wandering player. After we get settled, we will pay him to play for us," answered his mother.

The ladies made themselves comfortable on the rugs their servants spread under the trees. The children wandered about as they liked.

Ships in front of large city "IT LOOKED ALMOST LIKE A FAIRY CITY."
"Sweet Waters of Europe" is a good name for this part of the river. It was a pleasant place, and everything about them looked fresh and inviting.

"Osman, let's see what that man is showing," cried Selim, after the boys had listened to some music and eaten the ices they had bought at a stand.

The children joined a crowd of people gathering around a showman.

It was a puppet-show, something like the Punch and Judy one sees in England and America. But the funny little figures acted out a very different play. It must have been amusing, for every one laughed heartily.

Before the day was over other showmen came along, each with a different exhibition of his own. Then there were men who performed tricks, and others who had candies and dainties to sell.

As for the ladies, you must not think they sat quietly on their mats all day long. Oh, no indeed! They laughed and romped, they sang and danced, they ate candies and cakes as freely as the children themselves. The serious ways of the city were quite forgotten.

But at last the shadows of evening began to fall.

"Come, come, we must start for home," cried Osman's mother. "I must certainly be home by sunset to greet my husband."

They made haste to start, and in a few minutes they had taken their places in the boats and were moving back toward the great city.

As it came into view once more, it looked almost like a fairy city. The soft light of the late afternoon bathed the tall spires and minarets, which reached up toward the sky like long, slender needles.

Here and there were grand buildings of white marble, while the whole place was dotted with groves of dark cypress-trees.

Yes, it looked very, very beautiful, but when the boats were left behind, and the narrow, dirty streets were reached again, it did not seem possible it could be the same place the party had seen from the water.

There was no likeness to fairy-land now. The hungry dogs, the ragged beggars, the tumble-down houses in the very midst of the fine buildings, make the stranger feel sad.

But Osman is so used to these sights, they do not trouble him. This city, the greatest one of his people, always seems grand and beautiful to him.

On the evening after the picnic, Osman's mother said to her husband, "I have invited a party of my friends to lunch with me to-morrow."

The Turks do little visiting after sunset. The ladies often spend the day with each other, but are seldom away from home at dinner-time.

The next morning, after their master had gone away for the day, and Osman had started for school, the servants began to make ready for the party.

As soon as the first guest arrived, a pair of shoes belonging to Osman's mother was placed outside the door of her room. If her husband should happen to come home during the day, he would see these shoes. He would know by this sign that his wife had lady visitors. It would not be polite for him to enter her rooms during their stay in the house.

The lunch-hour soon came. The hostess led her friends into the dining-room. They seated themselves on the soft cushions placed by the servants around the low stand.

There was a spoon, and also a piece of bread, at each lady's place. On the centre of the stand was a leather pad on which hot dishes would be set as they were brought in. But when the ladies sat down there was no food to be seen, except the pieces of bread, some saucers containing olives, bits of cucumber, melons, and radishes.

And now the slaves moved from one guest to another, bringing a basin of water and towels. Each one must bathe her hands before eating, as well as afterward, whether alone or in the grandest company.

It was a pleasure to watch them. As the stream of clear water fell slowly into the basin, each one rubbed her fingers gracefully and daintily, and then dried them on the fine linen towel held out by the watchful servant.

When this had been done by every one, Osman's mother clapped her hands, and a tureen of thick, creamy soup was brought in and set on the leather pad.

The hostess politely waved her hand toward her principal guest. She was inviting her to be the first one to dip her spoon into the soup. After this, the other ladies joined in, all eating together from the same dish.

After a few mouthfuls, the hostess made a sign to the slave to remove the soup and bring in another dish. Before the meal was over there would be sixteen courses, at least, and, therefore, it would not be well to eat much of any one of them.

The guests ate a little of every course. But, between the courses, they nibbled at the olives, cucumbers, and different sweetmeats.

More than once, Osman's mother broke off a choice bit of food with her fingers, and held it up to the mouth of one of her friends. It was a very polite attention, and her visitor was pleased.

"How rude some people in the world are about eating," said one of the ladies. "They use the most clumsy things in their hands. They call them knives and forks. And besides, I have heard they do not wash before and after each meal. Ugh! It makes me shiver to think of their unclean ways."

"Yes, they are certainly not neat, and they are very awkward, if all I have heard about them be true," said another visitor. "They should study the ways of our people."

At last the luncheon was ended. The hostess led the way into the drawing-room, where coffee was now served.

They were having a merry time, laughing and chatting, when Osman entered the room. His face showed he had something he wished to tell. Making a low bow to the ladies, he turned to his mother and said:

"Oh, mamma, I just saw a cat fall ever so far. She was on the roof of that old building behind our house. She fell down, down to the ground. And, mamma, I thought she would be killed. But she came down softly on her feet and ran off as if she hadn't been hurt the least bit. How is it that a cat can do such a thing? No other animal is like her, I'm sure."

His mother laughed, and turned to one of her friends. "Won't you tell my little boy the story of Mohammed and the cat?" she asked. "We should all be pleased to listen, and perhaps there are some here who do not know it."

The rest of the company nodded their heads. "Yes, do tell it," said one after another.

"Very well, little Osman," said the lady whom the boy's mother had asked. "You shall have the story. I trust you will remember it whenever you think of the Holy Prophet.

"Mohammed once travelled a long, long distance over the desert. He became very tired, and at last he stopped to rest. As he did so, he fell fast asleep.

"Then, sad am I to tell it, a wicked serpent glided out from among the rocks and drew near the Prophet. It was about to bite him, when a cat happened to come along. She saw the serpent and what it was about to do; she rushed upon it and struggled and fought. The serpent defended itself with all its strength and cunning, too. Great was the battle. But the cat killed the snake.

"As it was dying, the wicked creature hissed so horribly that the noise awakened Mohammed, and he saw at once that the cat had saved his life.

"'Come here,' he said. As the cat obeyed him, the holy man stroked her lovingly three times. Three times he blessed her, saying these words:

"'May peace be yours, O cat. I will reward you for your kindness to me this day. No enemy shall conquer thee. No creature that lives shall ever be able to throw thee on thy back. Thou art indeed thrice blessed.'"

"And is this the reason a cat always falls on her feet?" asked Osman.

"Even so, my little friend. Perhaps after this story you will feel more loving toward those soft-footed creatures," said the lady.

Osman made a low bow and thanked her for her kindness in telling the story. He was about to leave the room when another of the visitors reached out her hand and softly patted his shoulder.

"Sit down beside me, my child. I have a story to tell the company. Stay and hear it, if your dear mother is willing."

"May I, mamma?" he asked.

"Certainly, Osman, if you are good and quiet."

The little boy at once settled himself beside the lady who had asked him to stay. This is the story he heard.

THE WOOD-CUTTER AND FORTUNE
Once upon a time there was a wood-cutter who lived in the forest with his wife and two children. He was very poor. Day after day, and year after year, he went out into the midst of the wood and worked hard chopping down the trees and cutting them up for fire-wood.

After he had cut all the logs he could fasten upon the backs of his two mules, he went with them to the nearest town and sold his wood.

As each year came to an end, the poor wood-cutter was no richer than he was at the beginning. When twenty such years had passed by, he began to feel quite hopeless.

"What is the use of working so hard?" he said. "Perhaps if I stay in bed from morning until night, Fortune will take pity on me. I will try it, at any rate."

The next morning, therefore, the wood-cutter stayed in bed, as he had promised himself he would do. When his wife found he did not get up, she went to wake him.

"Come, come," she cried, "the cock crowed long since. You are late."

"Late for what?" asked her husband.

"Late for your work in the forest, to be sure."

"What is the use? I should only gain enough to keep us for one day."

"But, my dear husband, we must take what Fortune gives us. She has never been very kind to us, I must admit."

"I am tired and sick of the way she has treated us. If she wishes to find me now, she must come here. I will not go to the wood to seek her any more."

When she heard these words, the woodcutter's wife began to weep bitterly. She thought of the empty cupboard. She was afraid of hunger and cold.

Neither his wife's pleadings nor her tears had any effect on the wood-cutter. He would not rise from the bed. In a little while a man came to the door of the cottage, and said:

"Friend Wood-cutter, will you help me with your mules? I have a load to move."

But the wood-cutter would not get up. "I have made a vow to stay in my bed, and here I shall stay," he answered.

"Then, will you let me take your mules?" asked the neighbour.

"Certainly, help yourself," said the wood-cutter.

The neighbour took the mules and went away. It happened that he had found a rich store of treasure in his field, and he needed the mules to carry it for him to his home.

But, alas for him! The animals were safely loaded and had nearly reached his house, when some armed policemen came that way. The man knew the law of the Sultan, by which he claimed all treasure-trove for himself.

There was only one thing for him to do, that is, if he did not wish to be killed for taking the treasure for himself. He must flee.

Away he ran as fast as he could move, leaving the mules to go where they chose.

You can easily guess they turned toward their own home. They soon reached it in safety.

When the wood-cutter's wife saw them standing in front of the door with their heavy loads, she rushed to her husband and begged him to get up and look into the matter.

But he still refused.

He had vowed to stay in bed till Fortune should visit him, and stay he would.

His wife, seeing something must be done, went out to the mules and began to cut the cords binding the sacks.

Of course you know what happened then. Out fell a perfect shower of gold pieces. The ground was soon covered with a golden carpet, richer than the most precious stores of the great East.

"A treasure! A treasure!" cried the woman, as she rushed to her husband's bedside. "Fortune has truly come to our home. Husband, you did right in waiting for her here. Look and see how rich we are now."

It was certainly time for the wood-cutter to get up, for he had kept his vow. As he looked at the piles of gold pieces, he said:

"I was quite right, dear wife. One must wait for Fortune. She is very fickle. You will never catch her if you run after her. But, if you wait for her, she will surely come to you."

When the story was ended, one of the ladies pointed to the clock.

"My dear friend," she said, turning to Osman's mother, "I have had a most delightful day. But it is now late in the afternoon. I must bid you farewell."

As she rose to go, the other ladies followed her example, each one thanking the hostess for the pleasant day spent with her.

CHAPTER V

GIPSIES

"I wish you had been with me this afternoon, Osman," said his father, as his little boy ran to meet him.

"What did you see, papa? Please tell me all about it."

"I went to walk with a friend. We wandered on and on until we came to a large field near the city walls. The field was alive with gipsies, who were having some sort of a holiday. They were dressed in their gayest colours and were having a dance."

"Outdoors in that field, papa?"

"Yes, Osman, and it was a very pretty sight. A number of the men were squatting on the ground in a circle. Those were the musicians. They played on different kinds of instruments. There were drums, flutes, and mandolins.

"The players banged away with no kind of time, but the gipsies seemed to enjoy it, notwithstanding."

"How did they dance, papa?"

"The men kept by themselves, each one moving separately. But the women danced together. They all beat time with their hands. At the same time they kept saying, 'Oh, Oh, Oh,' as they moved about.

"When the dance was ended, the gipsies went over to a corner of the field where a feast was being prepared. Great fires had been kindled. Huge kettles of rice were boiling there, and whole sheep were being roasted.

"Many of the young gipsies were handsome. Their eyes were dark and sparkling, and their teeth were of a pearly white. But the old women were wrinkled and ugly. Their long, thin fingers made me think of witches."

"The gipsies dress in the old style of our country, don't they, papa?"

"Yes, you always see them with large, baggy trousers, short jackets, and turbans wound around their heads. The men wear bright-coloured waistbands, stuck full of pistols and daggers."

"I feel scared, papa, only to hear you speak of such things."

"How foolish that is, Osman. The gipsies would do you no harm. They mind their own affairs pretty well. To be sure, we do not love these people, but there is nothing to fear from them.

"They have chosen to live among us, and, although they go away in large companies and travel all over Europe, they are sure to come back here."

"Where did they come from in the first place, papa?"

"A long time ago, I believe, they lived in the far East, or in Egypt. They speak a queer language, made up of Hindi and Greek, as well as Turkish words."

Just then, Osman's mother came into the room.

"Father has just been telling me about a feast held by the gipsies this afternoon, mamma."

"Indeed! And did any of the women offer to tell you your fortune?" asked the lady, as she turned toward her husband.

"They were having too good a time among themselves to notice any outsider," he answered. "At any other time I should have been bothered by them. I can't tell you how many times this year I have been asked to show the palm of my hand and cross it with silver."

"The silver is the pay for the fortune-telling, isn't it?" asked Osman.

woman reading another woman's palm "'SHE TOLD ME HE WOULD BE MY HUSBAND.'"
"Certainly; a gipsy wouldn't give you a moment of her time unless she were paid for it," said his mother.

"When I was a young girl, I loved to have my fortune told. One day a beautiful young gipsy girl came to the door of my house. Of course, she asked to tell my fortune.

"I spread out the palm of my hand and she looked at it a long time with her bright black eyes. She seemed to study the lines as though she were reading. At last, she began to speak slowly in a low voice. And, would you believe it! she described your father, Osman, although I had never seen him at that time. She told me he would be my husband."

Osman's father smiled a little and then said, "The less we have to do with these strange people, my son, the better. It is very easy for these fortune-tellers to make one or two guesses that afterward turn out to be true. But we have talked enough about the gipsies for one day. Let us speak of something else."

"Then tell me about our great ruler, whom you serve," said Osman. "I like to hear about the palace and the Sultan's little children who live in a city of their own inside of our great one."

The people of Turkey seldom speak of Osman's city as Constantinople, the name given it by the Christians. They prefer to call it "The Town."

"Yes, the palace and the buildings belonging to it really make a city by themselves," said his father. "It is a beautiful place, with its lovely gardens and parks. There is a lake in the midst of the park, and the Sultan sometimes sails around it in an elegant steam launch.

"The palace is of white marble, as you know, Osman. The furniture is of ebony inlaid with ivory. The curtains and carpets are of the brightest colours, and are rich and heavy."

"There is a theatre, as well as a great many other buildings, isn't there, papa?"

"Yes, Osman. It is decorated in the richest colours. The Sultan's seat is in the front part of the gallery."

"He has many children, hasn't he?"

"Yes, and he loves them dearly. He often spends the evening with them and plays duets on the piano with his favourites. The building where they live with their mothers is in the park. I have been told it is very beautiful."

"The Sultan has many, many wives, I have heard mother say."

"It is true. And each wife has a great number of slaves as well as other attendants. Sometimes his wives drive through the city in elegant carriages."

"But the Sultan never leaves the palace grounds, except on the two great times each year, does he?"

"Never, except at those times, Osman. But any one can get permission to see him as he rides on horseback to the mosque in his grounds, where he worships."

"It is a beautiful sight, papa. You know you have taken me there to see him. The lines of soldiers, all in red fezzes, reach from the door of the palace to the snow-white mosque. The Sultan himself looks so grand as he rides along!

"The troops cheer him as he passes them and enters the mosque, but everybody else is very, very quiet. I suppose they feel somewhat as I do, papa. I'm not exactly afraid. But he is such a great and powerful ruler, it doesn't seem as if I could move or make a sound while I look at him."

Dear little Osman! Our far-away cousin has never heard how the people of other countries speak of Turkey. They call it the "Sick Man of Europe." They think it is a pity the Sultan has such power in the land. They say:

"Turkey is the only country in Europe that does not believe in the Christian faith. Its most important city is on the shores of a strait through which a great deal of trade is carried from all parts of the world. These are some of the reasons different countries would like to get control of Turkey and its great city. They all look toward it with longing eyes.

"Besides these things, the Sultan himself is not a good ruler for his people. He has many wives and hundreds of slaves. Many of his people follow his bad example and buy slaves, both black and white."

But little Osman knows nothing of what is said about the Sultan and the people of his land. It has never entered his head that it is wrong to buy and sell human beings.

His mother is kind to her slaves, and does not make them work hard. Sometimes, too, she frees one of her slave women. They are happy, she thinks.

"But, dear little Osman," you would say, "it is the right of every one to be free. Perhaps when you grow up you will see this, and help to make things different in your country."

Let us go back now to the little boy and his father as they sat talking of the Sultan and his palace.

"He dresses very plainly," said the Turk. "But in the old days, the ruler's garments were very rich, and his fez fairly blazed with diamonds. If you had lived then, Osman, your eyes would have been dazzled when you looked at him."

"I wish I could have seen some of the things my grandmother has described," answered his son. "But I'm glad I wasn't living during the revolution of the janizaries. Everybody must have been scared then.

"Is it really true that Sultan Mahmoud's old nurse saved his life by hiding him away in an oven?"

"Yes, but he wasn't Sultan then. He was the heir to the throne, however."

"What made the trouble, papa?"

"Sultan Selim III. was a wise ruler. He wished to improve his country. At one time the janizaries were the best trained and most useful troops. They were chosen from the Christians who were taken captive in war.

"But after awhile, men with no training and with selfish motives managed to get into their ranks. Sultan Selim knew they were harmful to the Empire, and intended to disband them. They found out what he was about to do, took the city and palace by surprise, and killed the good Selim.

"As soon as his son's old nurse heard the uproar, she hurried to Mahmoud and said, 'Come with me at once; your life must be saved.' She led him to an old furnace in the palace and begged him to get inside.

"'No matter what happens, nor who calls your name, do not make a sound until I speak to you,' she told him.

"He did as she said. Hour after hour, he stayed quietly inside the furnace while his father and many of his friends were being cruelly killed.

"The Sultan's enemies hunted everywhere for him, but he was nowhere to be found. They called his name coaxingly, but he knew better than to answer any one else than his old nurse, so he did not make a sound.

"In the meanwhile, the old woman was patiently watching. When the janizaries had gone away, she went to the door of the furnace and whispered to Mahmoud. She told him he now had a chance to gather his men about him and seize the government.

"There was not a moment to lose; Mahmoud was quite a young man, but he had a strong nature. His wonderful eyes showed that.

"He came out from his hiding-place and succeeded in gaining control of the city. The wicked janizaries were conquered, but Mahmoud had a sad and troubled reign. Blessed be his memory!"

CHAPTER VI

A TURKISH BATH

"Osman, you may go with me to the public bath-house," said his father, one bright morning. "I have business at the bazaar to-day, and we will go there afterward. You can have a good bath."

Osman was delighted. A whole day with his father was a great treat. Besides, it pleased him to think of a visit to the public bath-house.

There was a large marble bath-room in his own home, and there were furnaces underneath to heat it. There were servants to wait upon him as he bathed. "Yet the public bath is better still," thought Osman, "and I love to go there." Probably you have all heard of Turkish baths. They are so delightful that people in America and other countries have copied them from the Turks. They have built similar bath-houses in their cities.

"Are we to drive or walk, papa?" asked Osman.

"We will drive. The carriage will be here in a few moments."

After a short drive they drew up in front of a large and handsome building. It was the public bath-house.

The first room entered by Osman and his father was a large hall. It was open overhead to let in the fresh air. There was a raised platform around the sides. This platform was covered with a soft carpet and divided into small dressing-rooms. Each visitor would have one of these for himself.

A fountain was playing in the middle of the hall, making sweet music as the water fell into the marble basin.

"Go into one of those little rooms and take off your clothing, Osman," said his father.

The little boy was soon ready for the bath. The attendant had wound three bright-bordered towels around him. One of these was tied about his waist, the second was twisted into a turban around his head, while the third one was thrown over his shoulders. He would not catch cold, for the towels were thick and warm. He wore wooden slippers on his feet.

Now for the warm chamber.

Osman knew what was coming. He went at once to the marble platform in the middle of the room. There he stretched himself on a soft mattress which the attendants placed for him.

They began to rub his feet and limbs very gently. How pleasant and restful it was! The little boy soon began to perspire. This was the time for moving him into a still warmer room, called the hot chamber.

Here Osman was rubbed briskly with a camel's-hair glove after a bowl of water had been poured over his body.

"Oh, how good this is," he thought, sleepily, when scented water was brought in, the attendant using the soft fibres of the palm in bathing him with the fragrant water. It was very, very pleasant.

There was no hurry. Hot clothing was laid on the boy when this last bathing was over; cold water was poured over his feet and he was taken to the cooling-room. Here he could lie on a soft, pleasant couch as long as he wished.

After a good rest, how the blood danced through every part of his body! Tired! It did not seem as though he could ever be tired again in his life. He was ready for any amount of walking and sightseeing.

"Father," he said, as they left the building and turned into one of the busiest streets, "I think a bath is one of the pleasantest things in the whole world."

"It almost makes a new man out of an old one," answered the serious Turk.

He never called himself a Turk, however. He would feel insulted to hear us speak of him in that manner. He would say, "I am an Osmanli, that is, a subject of the empire founded by Osman."

Osman, the founder of the empire, is also called Otman, so the subjects are sometimes spoken of as Ottomans, and their country as the Ottoman Empire.

Now let us go back to our little Osman and his father.

"See that poor beggar," whispered the little boy. "May I give him a coin, papa?"

It was a sickly-looking old man who filled Osman's heart with pity. He was very dirty, and his clothes were torn and ragged, although they were gay with bright colours. As he leaned against the side of a fountain, he made a picture you would like to paint. He kept crying, "Baksheesh, baksheesh," to the passers-by.

What a beautiful fountain it was! It had a wide roof, giving a pleasant shade. There were gilded gratings all around it, worked in lovely patterns,—roses and honeysuckles and trailing vines.

Brass drinking-cups, hanging around the sides, seemed to say, "Come, thirsty traveller, come and drink."

What a fluttering and cooing there was over the roof. At least a hundred pigeons were flying about, fearless and happy. No one would harm them, not even the ragged street boys who were playing about the fountain and ready for any mischief.

After Osman had given a silver coin to the beggar, his father pointed to the fountain, and said, "Look, my child, at the beautiful pattern of the grating."

"How pretty the gilded flowers are," answered Osman. "I love to see them. But, papa, there are ever so many fountains in our city. Nearly half of them are as pretty as this one. I believe there is hardly a street without one."

"I knew a very good man who died a few months ago. He left his money to be used in building a fountain. It was a kind deed. Don't you think so?"

"Yes, indeed, papa. There are always people and animals who are thirsty. It is a comfort to have fresh water at hand, especially if it is a warm day."

crowd of men in street "THROUGH THE CROWD OF BUSY PEOPLE."

As Osman was speaking, he heard a sound of music. Looking down the street, he saw two gipsies coming toward him. The man was playing on a bagpipe, and leading a tame bear. The woman was dressed in bright colours. She was beating a tambourine.

"Isn't it pretty music, papa? Oh, do look at the bear," cried Osman. "He is doing some tricks."

His father was in no hurry, so he and Osman joined the crowd who gathered around the gipsies. The bear danced in time to the music, and did other amusing things.

Osman tossed him a coin, which he carried to his master. This pleased the others, and they threw him some more coins.

"At this rate, the gipsies will go home to-night quite rich," laughed Osman's father, as they passed on. "We will go to the bazaar now. I must attend to some business there before it is much later."

"See that man with the tiger's skin over his shoulders," said Osman, a few minutes later. "He is clothed in rags, but he isn't a beggar, is he?"

"No, indeed, Osman. He is without doubt a wise man of our own faith, who prefers to be poor. He has probably come to the city to visit some holy tomb, in order to keep a vow he has made. He may have travelled many hundreds of miles. You should honour him, my little boy."

Osman and his father still moved through the crowd of busy people. They passed many Greeks and Armenians, who carry on a large share of the business of the city. There were also Englishmen and Americans, who were seeing the sights of this strange, lively place.

There were serious-looking Mohammedan priests in white and green turbans, with their eyes bent down to the ground. There were water-carriers with big jars on their backs, and sweetmeat-sellers with scales on which they were ever ready to weigh out the rich candies of Turkey.

As for dogs and beggars, there were hundreds of them, without a doubt.

"There is the bazaar, papa. I can see it on the hilltop beyond us."

It was an immense building of a brownish gray colour. You might almost call it a city in itself.

As Osman and his father began to climb the hill, they made their way between many stands and tiny booths where goods were for sale. Everything looked inviting, and Osman saw several things he wished to buy.

"See those lovely grapes, papa. I should like to carry some of them home," said the boy. But his father would not stop.

"We will not buy anything till we reach the bazaar," he said. "You will see enough there to tempt you, I do not doubt."

They passed on, and soon reached the entrance of the great building. It was quiet and dark inside, and there were many narrow little streets or passages, through which hundreds of people were moving. Each narrow passage was given up to the sale of some special thing.

The shopkeepers were from many different countries. There were shrewd Armenians, wily Greeks, Persians with big caps on their heads, and Turks with long beards, squatting comfortably by their counters.

The high roof was over all. Light was given by great numbers of little domes shining in every direction through this city of shops.

It was very pleasant to Osman. He liked to watch the crowds and look at the many lights. He enjoyed the strange odours of the East. He never grew tired of looking at the rich and beautiful goods for sale,—the goods of Europe, Asia, and Africa. Three continents seemed to meet in the great bazaar of Constantinople.

"Oh, papa, please look at these lovely stones. I should like to buy that necklace for mamma, she is so fond of amber."

But the boy's father replied, "Not to-day, Osman, not to-day."

Some queerly wrought swords now caught the boy's eye. They were made of the finest steel, and the handles were richly ornamented.

"How I wish I could have one of those for my very own, papa. Mayn't I please have one?"

"When you are a young man, Osman, we will look for the most elegant sword to be bought. But not now, my child."

Osman forgot his longing for a sword when he stood in front of a stand where perfumes were sold.

"We will buy some of this attar of roses. It will please your mother, and you may give it to her," said the father.

The Turks are fond of delicate perfumes, and there is none they like better than attar of roses, which is largely made in Turkey, and sent from there to other countries.

"Why does it cost so much?" asked Osman, as his father handed a gold coin to the shopkeeper.

"It is because only a few drops can be obtained from hundreds and hundreds of the flowers. Next year, you shall take a journey with me, Osman. I am going to the part of our country where the roses are raised for this purpose. It is a beautiful sight,—the fields thickly dotted with the sweet-smelling blossoms. You shall then see how the people get fragrant perfume from the flowers."

"I'm getting so hungry, papa. Can't we get some lunch? That cheese makes my mouth water."

A man with a round wicker basket containing different kinds of cheese was going through the street and calling his wares.

"Hush, Osman." His father pointed to the tower of a small mosque.

High up in this tower stood a man crying out to all faithful believers of Mohammed. It was the call to prayer.

Five times each day this prayer-caller mounted the tower. Each time he cried out to the people who were within reach of his voice.

Osman and his father instantly turned toward the sacred city of Mecca, and, kneeling down right where they stood, repeated a short prayer.

Then they slowly rose and turned their steps toward a restaurant, where they could get a delicious lunch.

There were many other peddlers in the streets besides the cheese-seller. Some of the shoppers bought what they wished from these peddlers. They could get unleavened bread or biscuits, custards, ices, sherbet, sweetmeats, hot vegetables, and many other things.

But Osman's father said, "We can be more comfortable in the restaurant. Besides, I should like a good dish of kebaby."

Kebaby! It was an odd name and an odd dish.

"It is very, very good," thought our little Turkish cousin, as he began to eat from the steaming soup-plate set before him.

The cook had placed tiny squares of unleavened bread in the bottom of the dish. Over this he had poured a quantity of sour cream, and last of all came little squares of hot meat. The dish was seasoned with salt, pepper, cardamom, and sumach.

"Good! Yes, very good," said Osman's father, as he tasted the kebaby. "There is nothing I like better."

When the lunch was over, he and his little son went to that part or the bazaar where carpets were sold. After many words about the price, a beautiful rug was purchased. Its colours were soft and rich. It was woven so closely it would last for many years. The shopkeeper had said it would be good for a lifetime, and he probably spoke the truth.

"Before we go home, will you take me out on the bridge of boats?" asked Osman. "It isn't far from the bazaar."

"Aren't you too tired?"

"No, indeed; the bath this morning made me ready for anything."

A short walk brought Osman and his father to the bridge of which he had spoken. It joins the main city of Constantinople and the suburb of Pera.

"It doesn't seem as though the bridge could be made of boats until we look over the sides, does it?" said Osman.

"No, dear. They are firmly chained together and covered with such strong planks that this bridge seems like any other. I must say I like to come here, myself. We can get such a fine view of the Golden Horn."

"Why do people call our harbour the Golden Horn?"

"It is shaped somewhat like a horn. Besides this, it is the channel through which many shiploads of the richest goods are carried. Think of the precious things you saw in the bazaar to-day, the beautiful gems, the spices, the silks, the shawls of camel's hair."

"I understand now. But look! There is a camel with a heavy load on his back. His master is leading him. I love camels."

"When I was a little boy," said his father, "my mother used to tell me stories of the old times. In those days there were none of the new-fashioned carriages in our streets. Only the gaily trimmed arabas, and sedan-chairs carried on men's shoulders could be seen."

"Mamma sometimes goes in a sedan-chair now," said Osman. "It must be a warm way of riding in summer-time, though. The close curtains keep out the air."

"You would have liked to see the camels in the old days, Osman. Merchants often travelled through the streets with whole processions of those animals. They went very slowly, to be sure, and they blocked up the streets. But camels are steady, faithful creatures, and are good beasts of burden."

"The dress of the people was much prettier long ago, wasn't it?"

"Indeed, it was. It is a shame so many of our people copy the fashions of other countries. The dress now looks stiff and ugly beside the loose robes and bright colours of the old times. But see, my child, the day has left us and I am tired. We must hasten homeward."

CHAPTER VII

THE WEDDING

"I wish I could have been there," thought Osman.

It was Friday morning, and the little boy was sitting beside his mother while she described the wedding-festival given in honour of two dear friends. She and her husband had spent all day Thursday at the bridegroom's house.

"It was a grand time, my little son. I wish you could have enjoyed it with us, but you were too ill to leave home," said Osman's mother, as she lovingly patted his cheek.

"Was there a great crowd, mamma?"

"Yes, indeed, for the young couple have hosts of friends. The ladies, of course, rode in carriages, and the men were on horseback. A band of music played lively tunes as we escorted the young bride to her new home.

"When we reached the house, the bridegroom stood waiting in the doorway. He led his bride to the bower in the bridal chamber, and, leaving her there, went to the 'place of greeting' to receive his gentlemen friends."

"You helped in making the bower, didn't you, mamma?"

"Yes. I went to the new home on Monday, with other friends and the relatives of the bride. The wedding-outfit and the presents had already been brought by some trusty porters.

"After we had refreshed ourselves with a lunch of coffee and sweetmeats, we began to decorate the bridal chamber. We hung the bride's pretty dresses, her shawls and prayer-carpet, her embroidered sheets and towels, on cords fastened along the walls.

"Then we chose one corner of the room for the bower. We hung up fine embroideries and festoons of gauze, and fastened numbers of artificial flowers here and there in the draperies. When it was done it was lovely!"

Osman's mother sighed with delight as she thought of it.

"But our work did not stop there, my dear. Oh, no. We placed the most precious wedding-presents in glass cases, so every one could see and admire them. Then we hung garlands of flowers on the walls of the room. It was very beautiful now.

"When this room was finished, we went into the next one and set up the new furniture and bedding, the beautiful candelabra, the smoking-set, and the kitchen ware."

"What did you do on Tuesday, mamma?"

"We went with the bride to the bath. When it was over, she put on borrowed clothing. Some bad fortune might come to her, if she did not follow this old custom."

"You spent Wednesday with the bride, too, didn't you?"

"Certainly, Osman. That is a very important day in the wedding-festival. I went to the bride's house quite early in the day, for we are very close friends. I helped her in receiving the bridegroom's mother and other relatives. All her special friends gathered there with me. We formed in a double row and helped the other guests up the stairs.

"I hope my dear Morgiana will be good friends with her new mother. As they sat side by side, the old lady passed sugar from her own mouth to that of her daughter-in-law."

"Why was that, mamma?"

"It was a token of the good feeling there will be between them, Osman."

"Dear me, a wedding-festival is a grand thing, isn't it? I wish I could have gone Thursday with you and papa. That was the greatest day of all."

"Yes, it was a very pleasant time for every one. There was an entertainment in the place of greeting for the men, and another for the women in the bride's rooms. Some gipsy girls danced and sang for us and we had refreshments."

"What was the bride doing all this time, mamma?"

"As soon as the bridegroom had led her to the bridal bower and gone away, her veil was raised. We could now look at her beautiful face as much as we liked, and admire her wedding-gown and presents."

"Did many poor people come in to look at the pretty things?" asked Osman. His voice was rather sad as he said the word "poor." He pitied those who did not have a lovely home like himself, and plenty to eat and to wear.

"It is so hard to be poor and have to work hard from early morning till late at night," he often thought.

"Yes, indeed, Osman. The house was filled with people all day long. No one was turned away from the door," answered his mother. "I saw women in shabby clothing standing beside the most richly dressed ladies. They seemed to enjoy the festival very much."

"When did the bridegroom enter, mamma?"

"As soon as the evening prayer had been recited in the 'place of greeting.' Then the bridegroom hurriedly left his men friends and started for the bridal bower."

Osman began to laugh. "I know what the men did then, mamma. I have heard papa tell about it. They pelted the bridegroom with old shoes and struck his back many a sharp blow. No wonder he hurried up-stairs as fast as he could go."

The boy's mother smiled. "And I can tell you what happened after the door closed behind him, although we visitors now took our leave. I well remember my own wedding.

"The bride kissed his hand as he entered. He knelt down on her veil and made a short prayer. After this a mirror was held in front of the young couple by an old woman friend of the bride, so they could see their faces in it side by side.

"Then sugar was passed from the young man's mouth to that of the bride. It was a symbol of the sweetness of their future life.

"But, my dear child, I have been so busy talking I did not notice the time. I must leave you to dress for the banquet at the home of our young friends. Run away and play with Selim."

CHAPTER VIII

THE CHILDREN'S CARNIVAL

"Selim, Selim, you will be late if you don't hurry," called Osman.

He himself had been ready for five whole minutes, and was becoming impatient because his little friend was not in sight. So he ran across the street to Selim's house to find out what was the matter.

"I will be dressed in a minute or two," said Selim. Osman sat down to count his marbles while he waited.

The two boys were going to a children's carnival in the grand courtyard of a certain mosque. Their mothers would go with them. Hundreds and hundreds of children would gather there to make the most of this glorious spring day.

Osman had looked forward to this festival for a long time.

"Isn't it beautiful?" he exclaimed, when he and Selim, with their veiled mothers, entered the courtyard and joined the crowd of happy little people.

The children played one game after another. The boys had their tops and marbles, and did many wonderful things with them. Of course, refreshments were plentiful; there were delicious sweetmeats, sherbets, and other things the children loved. And all the time the mothers, sitting on their gay carpets, watched the boys and girls at their play, and seemed to enjoy it as much as the little ones themselves.

"I have had such a good time," Osman told his father that evening. "Papa, do you remember when you were a little boy like me, and went to children's carnivals?"

"Yes, as if it were only yesterday, my dear. Yet many years have passed away since I romped with my boy friends and played with tops and marbles. But I have something else to speak of, Osman. Would you like to go with me to-morrow to the mosque of Agia Sophia?"

"Oh, papa, yes, indeed. I love to go with you anywhere. But it is so beautiful there, I shall be more glad than usual."

Osman's people use the word "mosque" as we do the word "church." Mosque means the place of prayer. The Turks build all their mosques in the same general way. They ornament them with domes and high-pointed spires called minarets.

When you visit Osman's home, you will see hundreds of these domes and minarets, for there are many mosques in his city.

"Papa, where is the oldest mosque in the world?" asked Osman.

"It is at Medina, in Arabia, on the very spot chosen by the great Prophet himself. A part of it is kept open to this day for all homeless people. That is, if they are believers in Mohammed. They can go there at any time and live in its shelter. It was the Prophet's wish."

"It would be nice if every mosque were like that one," said Osman. "When I grow up, I hope I may go to Medina and stand in the Mosque of the Prophet. He suffered very much, didn't he, papa?"

"A great, great deal," Osman's father sighed. "He received his teachings direct from Heaven. We find those teachings in the Koran, our sacred book.

"Mohammed had many enemies who believed he was cheating his followers. They did not believe that Allah (God) taught him. They even said bad spirits were the cause of his teachings. His life was in danger many times. But he and his teachings were saved."

view of mosque through archway "THEY CAME IN SIGHT OF THE MOSQUE AT LAST."
Osman's father bent his head, saying these words very slowly: "Allah is great, and Mohammed is his Prophet."

Osman repeated them after him. Then both father and son sat quiet for a few minutes. When the Turk spoke again, he said:

"It is bedtime for my little boy. Good night, my child." He bent down and kissed Osman, then motioned to his waiting nurse to go with him to his room.

The next day was clear and beautiful. Even the street dogs seemed quieter and happier than usual.

"It is good to be outdoors in the bright sunshine," said Osman, as he walked down the street with his father. They came in sight of the mosque at last. It was not beautiful to look at, but it was very, very large.

"Once there were no minarets rising from this mosque toward heaven," the boy's father told him. "Only the great dome reached upward from the roof. That was when the Christians ruled over our city and worshipped in this building. But when it came into our hands, many changes were made."

"Why do we call it 'Agia Sophia,' papa?"

"It is sacred to 'Wisdom,' my child. The way to wisdom must be through prayer. But here we are at the doorway."

Osman and his father hastily took off their shoes and put on the big, soft slippers handed them by an attendant. Other people, who were about to enter, did the same thing.

There was a good reason for this. The dust of the street must not be brought in to soil the floor or carpets. They must be kept clean. During the service the people bow their heads to the floor itself many times.

"It always makes me wish to be quiet when I go there," Osman once told his mother. "I wonder how men could ever build such a great, great place of worship."

There were no altars, no images, no seats. But along the walls, there were slabs of marble of all sorts and colours. Pillars of rare and beautiful stones held up the roof.

"They have been polished so they shine like mirrors," thought Osman, "and they are as beautiful as gems."

The floor of the mosque was strewn with prayer-rugs. They were arranged so the people who came to worship might all kneel toward the sacred city of Mecca.

"It is hundreds of years since Christians worshipped here," Osman's father had once told him. "They had altars of solid gold and shrines sparkling with precious jewels. Pictures of their saints were on the walls. But we, Osman, are taught not to have such paintings. A mosque should have no pictures of human shapes, nor of any other. For it is written: 'Thou shalt not make the likeness of anything.'

"When the great Sultan who conquered the Christians took possession of the city, he rode through this very building. It was crowded with people who had fled here for safety. The Sultan ordered that no blood should be shed. But he made the Christians the slaves of himself and his people.

"He changed the building into a place of worship fit for followers of Mohammed, saying, 'There is no God but Allah, and Mohammed is his Prophet.'"

"What was done with the altars and the images and paintings, papa?"

"The altars and images were torn down. The walls were covered with a coating of reddish plaster, even as you see them to-day, and this hid the pictures from sight."

"I love to come here in Ramazan. The brightness dazzles my eyes. I wish I could count the great wheels of light hanging from the ceiling at that time."

Ramazan is the only part of the year when the mosque is brightly lighted. It is a strange festival, and lasts a whole month.

The days are given up to fasting, and the nights to services in the mosques, to feasts, and frolics. It is the only time in the year when Osman's mamma leaves her home after the sun has set, and goes to evening parties of her friends.

All through the month, the streets are alive each evening with lights and processions and gay parties. But from dawn to sunset the followers of Mohammed must eat no food whatever, although they may feast all night long if they wish to do so.

Rich people, such as Osman and his family, enjoy turning day into night for a while. But it is not so easy for the poor, who must work without eating through the whole day, no matter how hungry and faint they may become.

CHAPTER IX

THE TWO FRIENDS

"Never forget your friends, Osman. I am glad you are so fond of Selim, although his family is poor. I hope you will always love him as you do now."

"Of course, papa. Selim is just like my brother. He always will be, too."

Osman looked up at his father with a little surprise. Forget Selim! He could not imagine such a thing.

"You ought to feel that way," said his father. "There is nothing so beautiful as friendship. I will tell you a true story about two boys who once lived in this very city."

Osman, with a happy smile, squatted on the rug by his father's side. There was nothing he liked better than a story.

"One of these boys," said the father, "was the son of a rich tobacconist. He was a Moslem, like ourselves, but his dearest friend was a little Armenian, whose father was a poor bread-seller and a Christian. The two boys were always together in work and play. After a while, their parents began to think, 'This is not good. A Christian and a Moslem should not be such close friends. We must not let this go on any longer.'

"Neither reasoning nor scolding did any good.

"At last the rich boy's father, the Moslem, decided to send him out of Turkey. 'It is the only way to make Ibrahim forget Joannes,' he said to himself. 'Ibrahim is now fifteen years old. He is nearly a man. Yes, I must send him so far away he will forget all about his Christian playmate.'

"Ibrahim was told of the plan. What did he do? He rushed to Joannes's home and said to his friend, 'I am going away, Joannes. I must bid you good-bye.'

"'No, indeed,' answered Joannes. 'Where you go, I will go, too.'

"'But that cannot be. My father has arranged it so that I go into another country. I am to serve the Pasha of Bagdad. But I shall never forget you, Joannes. And when I come back to this city, I shall come as your true and loving friend.'

"The two boys embraced and kissed each other. Then Ibrahim went away. Soon after this he was sent far away to the city of Bagdad.

"He served the pasha so well that he soon held a high position. Years passed away and the pasha died. A surprise was now in store for Ibrahim. He himself was made pasha.

"But he longed for his old home. He wished to see his friend Joannes once more, for he had never been forgotten. He sent word to the Sultan, asking if he might visit this city for a short time.

"But the Sultan said, 'No; the country needs your care. Stay there and keep it in order.'

"More years passed away. Again the pasha asked permission to leave Bagdad that he might visit his old home. And again the Sultan refused.

"Soon after this, a strange thing happened. The Sultan became angry with his chief officer, the Grand Vizier. He had his head cut off, and, would you believe it, he sent for Ibrahim to come here to be Grand Vizier in his place.

"Ibrahim was hardly settled in his high position before he sent two of his body-guard to the narrow street where his old friend used to live. They were told to find him and bring him before their master.

"When they came to the little store of the bread-seller, they went inside and asked for Joannes.

"He came forward in a great fright. What had he done that the Grand Vizier should send for him? He trembled as he declared he had done no wrong to any man, neither theft nor murder,—no harm whatever.

"But the officers would not listen. Their master had ordered Joannes to be brought to him, and they must obey his command.

"He must go. There was no help. Joannes sent a sad farewell to his wife and children, for he fully expected he was about to meet death. His pitying friends and neighbours crowded around as he went with the officers from his little store.

"They brought him into the presence of the Grand Vizier. But poor Joannes did not dare to look in his face. He threw himself face downward on the floor, and begged that his life should be spared.

"'Arise!' said the Grand Vizier. 'I do not wish you harm. I want to talk with you. Do you remember Ibrahim, your boy friend?'

"'Remember him! I loved him above all others. But he went away, and I never saw him again.'

"'I am he,' answered the great man, and he fell on Joannes's neck and kissed him. Then he reminded Ibrahim of the last words spoken before they parted.

"'I am still your friend,' he said. 'Behold, I will show you that I am.

"He sent for his accounts, and then and there made Joannes his chief banker. He gave him charge of all his money. He sent him home in a grand uniform, on a fine horse, and with servants to attend him.

"You can imagine the surprise of Joannes's wife when he came home in such style.

"No, he had not been killed, after all. The poor woman fainted with joy at the glad sight. But she soon came to her senses, and both she and her husband lived to enjoy the loving kindness of Joannes's old friend, now the Sultan's highest officer.

"That was friendship worth having, indeed."

"What a lovely story, papa. Maybe I shall grow up to show Selim how much I love him, too."

"It may be. Yes, it may be so. Or, possibly, Selim will have the chance to show you how deeply he cares for you, Osman. Who knows what changes will come to our country? Who knows, indeed!"

Osman's father became silent as he thought of the enemies of Turkey, and of what might happen to his loved country if they should band together against the Sultan and his power.

THE END